Swift Justice

By

Charlie Skinner

Monaco-Italy

The warm sea air fluttered across the tourist woven beach as the blistering red sun set into the ocean. The evening light cast large shadows on the towering mansions that surrounded the coast. The largest mansion belongs to the kingpin of drugs throughout the world Sal Desoto. The lavish mansion sits like an emerald in the sky expensive cars sit outside as the sixteen foot high metal gates protect it like the gates of Heaven. Heavily armed men patrol the outside, their presence alone tells intruders to stay away. Sal Desoto is a gray haired bulky man who has seen his fair share of skirmishes. Rising from a poor family to become the most wanted drug lord in the world was no easy task but Sal took on the challenge in a violent non forgiving way that allowed him to rise to the top and now at 62 he presides over everything and anything.

Desoto's marbled filled mansion is filling with laughter as he parties on his lavish terrace with two beautiful girls. Wine bottles lay on the floor along with anything the girls had previously been wearing. A sharped dressed butler strolls on to the terrace and reluctantly interrupts the party. The butler proclaims, "Mr. Desoto, I'm sorry to bother you but Mr. Julian is here to see you. He says it is very important." Desoto raises an eyebrow motions to the butler with a nod that he understands, "okay, all right ladies we'll continue this party later." The girls bounce out of the hot tub giving Desoto a kiss as they leave. Desoto heaves himself out grabbing his robe and tightening the string. The butler continues, "Mr. Julian is waiting in your office sir."

Desoto and the butler descend into the house. The marble floors and art work make the place look like an ad for only the finest things in life. The two approach a very large wooden door and the butler opens the door and Desoto makes his way into his office. The butler closes the door and continues on with his day. The lavishly furnished office contains a very large mahogany desk; the desk sits by a window overlooking the bay. A big couch and silk lined chairs fill out the room. A young man dressed in a suit pours a glass of scotch as he sees Desoto walk in; he starts to pour another one. Vin Julian is the man he is Desoto's right hand guy. Vin starts out, "Mr. Desoto I'm sorry to bother you but we have a problem." Desoto takes his drink and sits down taking a long slow sip of the well-aged scotch Desoto says, "Talk to me Vin." Vin straightens his tie and begins, "It seems we have a problem. The boys over the pond want to completely cut off their ties with us. They say we aren't involved anymore and that we are just taking our cut without doing any of the leg work." Desoto's face becomes flush with anger; he stands up violently and throws his drink to the ground. The glass shatters sending scotch covered ice cubes and glass careening all around. Vin nervously sets his drink down. Desoto clenching his fist exclaims, "Aren't doing our leg work, who the fuck started the drug business in New York, who the fuck made all the connections, I'm the fucking kingpin of crime there. If it weren't for me they'd be still petty fucking thieves. Just because I left the country they get big fucking heads."

Vin slowly sets his drink down, "They said their through with us and we shouldn't show up to the annual meeting, cause if we do we're dead." Desoto is now beaming wit hanger as he kicks over a chair and heads to look out the window. Desoto declares, "We're dead, fuck them their dead." Vin now feeling uncomfortable about his own future stands up and approaches Desoto, Vin finding his words, "What the hell we going to do? They'll kill us as soon as we get off the plane. They'll be watching like hawks." Desoto gets a smile on his face and heads over to his phone. He picks it up and grins, "I'm going to send in my angel." Vin starts to laugh, "I didn't know God was working for the mob, he got some angel of death?" Desoto starts to dial and says, "They're going to wish he did cause my angel doesn't forgive."

New York City

The lights are lighting up the midnight sky as 747 airplane starts to make its decent into the airport. The first class section of the plane is starting to buzz with passengers longing to feel land again after a long flight. A welcoming voice comes over the loud speaker as stewardesses start preparing for the landing, "We are now landing in New York, thank you for flying with us tonight I hope you enjoy your stay."

Dominique Sloan sits waiting to get off. She is young, beautiful and very intelligent with model looks and an athletic build to go along; she is wearing a black summer dress and an overcoat. She sits in the seat by the aisle, looking ready to get off a focused look is on her face. A sleazy business man sitting by her leans over and says, "So you here for business or pleasure? Cause if it's pleasure I'm your man." Dominique turns and looks at the man. She slowly pulls her sunglasses down and looks him up and down. Business man, "So what do you think?" Dominique smiles and replies, "If you weren't so pathetic I'd feel bad about this." She takes the half-filled drink still sitting in front of the man and dumps it on his lap. The business man pushes back in his chair, "You dumb bitch!" He grabs her arm and her coat flies open revealing a 9mm pistol. The businessman says, "You some kind of cop?" Dominique stares him down, "No, cops care." She snaps her wrist and a mini gun slides into her hand. She sticks the gun in his crotch. Businessman replies, "You're fucking crazy!" He gets a panicked look on his face as Dominique leans over and whispers in his ear, "What's the matter don't I make you hot?" She pulls the trigger and the gun is a lighter. The flame comes out and his pants light on fire.

The plane is now stopped and the passengers are getting their belongings. Dominique grabs her bag from the overhead and leaves down the aisle. The business man continues to tap at the fire to put it out, as passengers start leaving the plane they stare at him.

A black limousine is parked outside. A chauffeur waits holding a sign that reads D. Sloan. He stands leaning against the car when he sees Dominique walking out. The chauffeur quickly comes to attention. Chauffeur, "Miss Sloan, how are you doing this evening?" Dominique stops and surveys the area and replies, "Just fine, do you know where I'll be going?" The chauffeur starts to open the door and begins, "Mr. Desoto has instructed me to take you to the Plaza Towers." Dominique gets in and the Chauffeur closes the door. He heads to the driver's side and gets in. The limo pulls out into the gridlock.

Dominique is getting comfortable in the back. She pours herself a drink and starts to open her bag. The bag contains numerous throwing knives and guns. Everything one would need to start a personal war. She raises her dress and removes a gun she had strapped to her leg and puts it into the bag. She stares out the window as other cars go by the bright lights of the city lay off in the distance almost like a signal for what is to come. Just as Dominique begins to doze off a ringing can be heard from her bag. She reaches in and pulls out her cell phone. Dominique, "Talk to me." It's Mr. Desoto on the other end. Desoto," Dominique, I take it you made it all right." She stares out the window while she talks, "The plane ride was a little hot." She says as she flicks the gun lighter in her hand. Desoto continues, "Your base will be the Plaza, the meeting of the families is at the museum. "How quaint." she replies. Desoto continues," The meeting will take place on Saturday evening. The guards there are on the take. The only people that will be there are the Diablo family and the Valones. Vinni Valone is the man I want killed. We have to take back what was ours.

He seems to think he's the one running the show, we take him out the rest will fall." Dominique sits listening as she spins on the silencer for her 9mm pistol and points it at the driver's seat. "What if I get a little trigger happy?" She inquirers. Desoto replies, "Trigger-happy is not a bad thing. You just kill that son of a bitch Valone and anything else that gets in your way just consider it target practice." Dominique puts the gun into her bag, "That's music to my ears." She says as she turns off the phone and puts on some headphones as the limo continues on its journey.

Plaza Hotel

The hotel is busy. People are outside, people are going in, cars are being parked. From above it looks like a bee hive with all the activity that is going on. The limo carrying Dominique pulls up to the front and the driver gets out, he opens the door and Dominique makes her way out. The diver says as he holds the door, "Enjoy your stay Miss Sloan." Dominique looks at him for a minute, as if he knows too much. The driver continues in a flirtatious many, "I hope to see you again." Dominique kisses two of her fingers and presses them against his lips. The driver stumbles back against the limo. Dominique, "It wouldn't be healthy for you to see me gain. I'm a real killer in bed." It's almost a warning to him as she senses something could be up. She turns and picks up her bag and walks away. The driver smiles as she leaves. He waits till Dominique is inside the hotel then the driver pulls out his phone and starts to dial.

Valone Townhouse Manhattan

The townhouse contains an enormous living room by Manhattan standards, with a view that overlooks the park. Exotic art hangs on the walls and the expensive furniture shows the money of the owner. Vinni Valone has been spending his take of the money on the finer things in life and it shows. The well-built fifty year old has worked his way up the same way as Desoto but now he wants it all. The jacket of his fine pin striped suit hand in his plush office where Valone is doing some paper work. His phone starts to ring and he picks it up. Valone, "This is Valone, what you got?" It's the limo driver on the other end. Driver, "Mr. Valone this is

Chris. I picked up Dominique Sloan that is who Mr. Desoto told me to pick up. He has no idea I'm calling you, he still thinks I'm working for him sir." Valone turns in his chair trying to recall the name of Dominique Sloan he pauses and then responds, "Sloan, where is she staying?" The driver continues, "She's at the Plaza and she is alone." Valone leans back in his chair and starts to formulate a plan. Valone, "All right come back here. I'm going to have you pick up some of the boys then you guys can pay her a visit." Valone hangs up the phone and says to himself,"Damn it."

Valone gets up from his desk and heads for the door. He exits the room and heads down the painting filled hall way. He is on his way to the main room in the house. There are about ten people in the room all dressed in suits. They vary in age and some are smoking cigars. Whiskey bottles and scotch bottles are on the main desk in the well-furnished room. The sweet smoke of the cigars curl up and fill the room as the clanging of glasses can be heard. The guys are sitting around talking. John Diablo, the leader of the other mob is there. He stands out from the rest by his towering presents and massive frame. His mop of hair makes him look younger than he is. Valone finally makes his way to the room and walks in. Some of the chattering stops and Valone goes to the desk and takes a seat. He pours himself a drink and starts, "Listen up, I just got a call from Desoto's driver. It seems the fat bastard didn't have the balls to show up himself, some girl named Dominique Sloan got in the car." Valone takes a long drink and stares around the room to see if anybody has an idea. Diablo rubs his chin trying to come up with something he says, "Sloan. Why does that sound familiar?" Valone knew the whole time who Dominique was, he just wanted to see if anyone else could recall. Valone, "I'll tell you why; Dominique Sloan is the daughter of Richard Sloan. Desoto's old right hand man before I killed him to take over." Diablo is now remembering, he takes a long draw from his Cuban cigar and says, "That was seventeen years ago, Desoto never knew. He thought it was a deal that went bad." Valone nods his head and stands up, "That's when Desoto left the country, it was a promise to Richard that if anything happened he would raise Dominique since her mother was dead. Desoto thought it would be best if she wasn't around all the violence. But that move cost him his empire because we aren't going to do the legwork anymore." Diablo taking a puff from his cigar, "So why did she come back? Her mother passed away when she was little, he has nothing here." Valone slowly walks over cutting a tip of a cigar he stand in front of Diablo and leans down, "Who gives a fuck, cause she's going back in a bag. You guys get ready you're going to the Plaza." The men start to get ready as Valone and Diablo plot out the plan and start to give the orders.

Plaza Hotel

A lot of people are walking around. The bellhops are carrying luggage and Dominique is at the front desk. She has just finished checking in. The desk clerk says, "Here you go Miss Sloan, take the elevator to the twentieth floor. I hope you enjoy your stay." She hand the key card to Dominique and smiles. Dominique takes the card and replies, "Thank you I'm sure I'll have an explosive time." The clerk smiles and Dominique walks toward the elevator. She reaches the elevator and presses the up button. Dominique gets bumped into the door; she quickly turns to see who hit her. It's a young couple that has just gotten married and they are on their honeymoon. The couple is kissing and obviously can't wait to get to their room. The young bride laughing and hugging her husband, "We're sorry." Dominique," That's all right. Looks like you're going to have some fun tonight." Dominique looks into the couple's bag which just happened to be open revealing a bottle of wine, handcuffs and a whip. The bride notices and her face flushes red and she says embarrassingly, "Yea, it was a long ceremony." The groom kissing his wife leans over and adds, "Yea, too long." Dominique smiles and turns toward the elevator door which is now opening.

The three walk in and Dominique pushes the number twenty on the control panel. She ask the couple what floor they are looking for the groom fumbles to find his card and looks at it," Twenty." he says with a smile. Dominique just smiles as the door closes and they start their assent upward. The elevator door opens. Dominique and the couple walk out. There is a maid in the hall cleaning another couple waits to get in the now empty elevator. Dominique walks toward her room which happens to be right next to the couples. The bride comments, "Is this a coincidence or what?" Dominique smiles as she inserts her card, "You guys have fun tonight." The couple opens their door too busy now to hear what anybody is saying they continue to make out as they enter their room. The room is very plush and first class the windows overlook the city and the bright lights and street noises seem to fade away. A complementary bottle of wine is on ice. She hears a bang on the wall from the couples room and smiles as she throws her gear onto the bed. Dominique is relieved to finally be there and sits on the edge of the bed, "What am I getting into," she says to herself.

Outside the Plaza a limousine pulls up carrying Valone's men. Chris the chauffeur gets out along with three other men. They look around and start to walk in. Chris is straitening his tie as he walks, "I'll find out what room she is in." He says to the others. Dominique is putting her bag under the bed. She slips off her dress and is wearing a thong and a small top revealing her beautiful body. She walks over toward the shower and turns it on. Chris along with the three other men are standing in the hall outside her room. One of the guys starts to turn the handle slowly, "Its locked." He whispers. Chris looks around, "I'll just knock and tell her she left something in the car." He knocks on the door. Dominique hears the knock and turns off the water not expecting anyone she is surprised. She leaves the bathroom and heads toward the door. "Who is it?" She says. Chris is now motioning the guys away from the peep hole in the door, "It's me, Chris, Miss Sloan. I'm sorry to bother you; you left something in the car." Beads of sweat are building on Chris's forehead, "I thought I would return it for you. I hope it's not a bad time?" He continued. "Okay, just a minute." Dominique says as she approaches the door. She looks through the peep hole in the door. She sees Chris standing but nothing is in his hands. She realizes he is here for something else probably trying to get a date or some action. Dominique shakes her head, "I'll be right there." She hears Chris reply, "I'm really glad I caught you here yet." Dominique unlocks the door and heads back toward the bed where her dress is, "What an asshole." She mutters. Chris hears the door unlock and signals to the other guys to get ready. One of them puts on leather gloves. The second man wraps his hand with a chain and the third man pulls out a silencer and puts it on his gun. Chris grabs the handle and starts to turn the knob slowly. The handle in the room starts to move. Dominique sees the handle turn and now realizes this isn't going to be a friendly visit. She throws her dress down as the door opens and reaches for her bag. The bag is just out of her reach. "Shit!" she exclaims. It's too late now. Chris is coming through the door with the others. Dominique gets up and smiles.

Chris pulls out a big buck knife and smiles, "Baby I knew you wanted me. Love hurts." He begins to wave the large knife side to side. Dominique responds, "Don't you remember, I'm a killer in bed." She walks from behind the bed and pulls the sides of her G-string up in a sexy manner to get him to look. Chris looks her up and down and licks his lips, "What a shame." He says. Dominique stands in front of him and blows Chris a kiss. She then kicks his hand which is holding the knife and sends it right into his throat. Chris drops to his knees and she pulls the knife out. Blood flows from his neck like as wave of red hot lava as he grabs his throat trying to stop the flow. "What's the matter foreplay a little too rough?" Dominique says with a grin of delight. She grabs the wine bottler as the other three guys surround her. The one with the gloves is on her right. The man with the chains stands by her left. The guy with the gun is in front still fumbling with the silencer. "Come on let's party." She says. Dominique tosses the bottle and catches the small end holding it like a club. She hits the guy on the left. The bottle explodes sending him down like a ton of bricks in a shower of blood and glass. He falls against the door that separates the rooms from one another. She jams the buck knife into the thigh of the guy with the leather gloves. He clutches at the knife. The guy with the gun finally has the silencer on and points the gun at Dominique. The gunman points the gun,"Fuck you bitch!" He squeezes the trigger but the safety is on. Dominique inquires," Need some help?"

She grabs his wrist and twists it so the gun is pointing toward him. She winks at him as she clicks the safety off and pulls the trigger sending five bullets into him. He falls back into the hall in a bloody heap. The man who got hit with the bottle stands up and staggers toward Dominique, she pulls the trigger but the gun jams. "We'll have to do this the hard way." Dominique says. She throws the gun down and the man takes a swing, she ducks and knees him in the groin then uppercuts him. Blood and teeth come flying out from the violent blow. She grabs him and throws the man against the door that separates the two adjoining rooms. Dominique throws five hard punches to his face and turns it into a bloody pulp. She backs away and the man smiles a bloody toothless grin. He replies, "That all you got?" She steps back and jump kicks him in the middle of the chest.

The married couple is on their bed. He is handcuffed to the bed and she is on top with a whip, he has a gag in his mouth. Just then the gunman comes crashing through the door from Dominique's kick. The couple immediately stop and look on in shock at what is happening. They were oblivious to anything that was happening next door but not now. Dominique comes walking through the entrance as the door hangs on a whimpering hinge. "Mind if I join in." She says. The couple is wide eyed, the groom's eyes light up, every man's dream is about to come true. Dominique grabs the whip the gunman gets to his feet. She snaps the whip around his neck and pulls him to the balcony. Dominique grabs on to the whip with both hands. She pulls him toward the railing the force propels him over the top. The gunman lets out a final scream as he plunges to his death.

Dominique walks back into the room. The couple is still speechless; the couple is now off the bed and wearing robes, Dominique hands them the whip. "Maybe next time we can go a little soft-core. By the way if anybody asks where I am tell them I never went to my room. Tell them I came back after it happened and saw the mess and left. I would hate to have to come back." Dominique says with a grin as the couple nods still in shock. Chris is still on the floor barley alive. The man with the knife in his leg is hiding in the bathroom. Dominique walks back into her room. She looks around. She sees Chris and picks him up by the shirt to look in his eyes. As she looks she sees a refection in his eye of the knife guy coming up behind her. Dominique spins Chris around just as the man plunges the knife at her. The knife sticks right into Chris's back as he drops to the ground dead. The knife man backs up. "I'm really tired." Dominique says. The guy lets out a yell as he charges, she ducks and he goes over her, falling over the bed. He looks up frantically then sees Dominique come up from the other side of bed holding her gun. "Fuck you." He says. Dominique replies, "Whatever you say." She pulls the trigger unloading the whole clip into his chest and face. He goes crashing through the doors leading to her balcony. Sirens are starting to blare across the city and the hotel alarm is sounding.

Dominique slips on her dress and starts to gather her stuff. The hotel is now in full chaos mode. People are coming out of their rooms to see what is going on. Dominique gets lost in the confusion and heads for the exit. Fire trucks and police cars are roaring toward the hotel. People are running around outside amid all the madness. Dominique makes her way toward the back exit and heads out onto the street as the police come rushing past her to get inside. An officer shouts out, "Please head away from the premises, over to the police cars. We need to ask questions." It's now mass confusion outside as news crews and crowds are starting to gather. Dominique continues to blend into the crowd and eventually crosses the street away from the mayhem.

As she passes a store a news report comes on a television. A reporter is outside the hotel and begins, "This is Krissy Tomblin reporting live from the Plaza hotel. Were earlier tonight a shoot-out occurred on the twentieth floor. Details are not being released but it is said four people are dead. As soon as we get more information I'll bring it to you. This is Krissy Tomblin reporting for channel 7 news."

Valone Townhouse

Vinni Valone walks away from the television after hearing the report. Diablo is sitting in a chair having another drink. Valone, "You believe this shit? We send them over there to kill one lousy girl and they get whacked." He continues to pace the floor. Diablo interjects, "What are we going to do?" Valone is growing frustrated, "We are going ahead as planned. The meeting will take place so we can gain full power of this organization." Diablo looks up and says, "What if the other guys wonder what happened?" Valone pours himself another drink and replies, "We'll just say a deal went bad. They don't have to know about Miss Sloan. If she tries and crashes our meeting she'll meet the same fate as her dad.

Ally Just Past the Hotel

Dominique looks around to make sure she wasn't followed. She pulls out her phone and starts to dial. As the phone rings she studies her minor injuries she sustained during the fight. The phone is answered by Desoto. Dominique, "Its me, there was a little problem." Desoto responds, "What happened?" Dominique continues to look around and leans against the wall. Dominique, "Valone knew I was here they tried to kill me." Desoto," Chris must have ratted you out, how many were their?" Dominique continues, "Four, Chris thought he was the man and two thought they were invincible. The other one thought he could fly. They were all wrong." Desoto, "Where are you now?" She looks around and takes in the area one more time and says, "Just an ally down from the hotel." Desoto responds, "You remember my cousin Gino? His town house is empty right now; I'll give him a call. He will send someone over to open it up for you. You can stay there for the night. You remember where it is?" Dominique thinks a minute then remembers, "Yes, I remember." Desoto continues, "Okay, they probably won't send anybody for you tonight as they don't want to draw much attention that I sent someone. Stay with the plan. Kill every one of those bastards."

Rain starts to fall. Dominique replies, "I'll call you when it's done." She turns off the phone and grabs her bag and heads toward the street. A cab pulls up and she gets in as the light of the street lamps lead the way.

Gino's Manhattan Townhouse

Morning has arrived and the plush house with nice furniture and art work is a welcoming change for Dominique. The television is on and Krissy Tomblin is back reporting. Krissy, "This is Krissy Tomblin here at the Plaza. Where last night what appeared to be a botched drug deal has left four dead. The couple next door says the woman next to them was out. The next thing they were awakened by gunfire wand their door was being broken down. Police say the men probably found an empty room and used it for the deal. The couple says the women returned to the room to find the bodies. She panicked and left with everyone else when the building was evacuated. Police are looking for any information, back to you Steve." The anchorman comes on and says, "I wouldn't pay full price for that room."

As this is going on Dominique is in the shower.

She gets out and studies the bruises on her back and arms from the fight. She grimaces as she gets dressed. She is starting to feel the effects from last night. She slowly rubs her back with her hand when she hears a noise. She throws on her shirt and pants and then grabs her gun. Dominique slowly opens the bathroom door. She looks down the hall and sees nothing but hears more noises. Dominique starts to walk down the hall. She holds her gun out and makes sure it is loaded. The noise is now getting louder and it is coming from the kitchen. Trying to be as quiet as a cat she glides into the kitchen. She sees a young man, kind of heavy with black hair slicked back. He is wearing baggy shorts and a flower shirt. It's Gino's nephew Paul. A real laid back person that trusts everyone. He has brought some food for Dominique at his uncle's request. Paul has a big box of donuts that he has already been eating. He takes another bite and turns around. He is met with Dominique's gun barrel stuck into his mouth. "I wouldn't bite down if I was you, the next bite might be hard to swallow." She says. Paul begins to mumble as the food and gun impair his speech, "I'm Uncle Gino's nephew Paul." He tries to say. Dominique's concern leaves her now as she is not threatened by him anymore. "I'm going to pull this gun out. If you want to taste that next bite don't be stupid." She says. Dominique removes the gun from his mouth. Paul finishes chewing and starts, "I'm Uncle Gino's nephew how you doing?"

He grabs her and gives Dominique a hug. She starts to shake he head at this character and is relieved he is friendly. "Okay, okay." she says as she pushes him away. Paul continues, "I was told to come here and make sure you were all right and bring some food." He starts to pour a glass of milk which he got from the refrigerator. "So everything all right? If you need to know anything I'm your man." Paul says. Dominique sits down and looks at the donuts. "Listen, Paul how about we go out for breakfast?" She says. Paul gets a big smile on his face. Seeing he is never one to turn down an invitation to eat replies, "Sounds great I know a little place down the street. You know I never like to miss breakfast it's

very important." Paul continues to carry on Dominique
pushes the donut box aside and say, "Let's go "Paul."
They head out to the street. The morning rush is beginning.
People and cars are everywhere. Shops are opening and
setting up their outside displays. They walk into a quaint café
and sit down.

Valone Townhouse

Valone is sitting behind his desk talking on the phone.
There is another man in the room. He is Mr. Marcus,
Valone's enforcer. He is a muscular black man who looks like
he could knock down a brick wall just by leaning against it.
Mr. Marcus sits in front of Valone polishing a .50 Caliber
pistol. Valone hangs up the phone and says, "That was
Diablo, everything is a go for tonight. Just one last detail has
to be dealt with. Miss Sloan is still out there and she could be
a problem. Mr. Marcus, you're my problem solver see what
you can do." Mr. Marcus stands up filling up the room. He
puts his gun holster on and says, "Dead or alive?" Valone
starts to smile and replies, "Use your better judgement." Mr.
Marcus stats to grin and says, "Consider the problem dealt
with." Valone nods in agreement and says, "Take the car and
some men. Then come back and we'll head to the meeting."

Café

The café is about half full. Dominique and Paul are
sitting at a little round table. They are almost done eating;
their plates are just about empty as they talk. "What do you
do Paul?" Dominique inquires. Paul whips his mouth and
starts, "I work for my uncle, I'm kind of the man on the street.
I keep him informed on what's going on." He looks around
and leans over table and whispers, "Don't think I don't know
why you're here. That was your handy work the other night at
the Plaza wasn't it?" Dominique starts to smile, "You seem to
have done your homework." Paul responds, "Listen I might

have something you'll be interested in. It's not quite the army but I think it might help you with your problem."
Dominique's eyes light up and she says, "What would that be?" Paul now getting full of himself, responds "I just happen to have access to the biggest fucking vault of weapons you'll ever see. I can get you in and all those toys will be at your disposal." Dominique, "I never turn down a shopping spree." Paul starts to nod his head in agreement, "Let's rock and roll." Dominique and Paul get up. Paul takes a couple more bites then finishes off his juice. He reaches into his pocket and pulls out a roll of money. He peels off a hundred and throws it on the table, "It's on me." They head for the exit.

Outside the activity has died down. As they walk out a black car drives by slowly with tinted windows. Dominique stares at the car as it slows down. Paul continues to talk as the car pulls ahead of them and slams on the brakes. Dominique, "I think we've got a problem, its Valone's men." Paul stops and looks, "Oh shit, let's go!"

The car comes screeching back in reverse. The windows are coming down. A machine gun barrel comes out the window and starts to blast away. Shells are filling the street and the thunderous sound is exploding all around. Dominique and Paul drop behind a parked car as the windows are being blown out. They cover their heads as bullets and glass rain down over them. People on the street start running for cover.

Dominique pulls out her 9mm. "We need a ride." She says. Paul yelling over all the noise, "Down there, we'll use that car." He points down the alley at a car that sits at the ends of the street. It would be at the back of the café. The streets run on both sides of the building. The car is a brand new yellow corvette. Dominique yells, "Can you hot-wire it?" Paul responds, "It was my hobby growing up." Dominique says, "We'll make a run for it." She stands up and fires a few rounds of love into the car. The shooter drops the gun. Dominique and Paul take off running for the corvette. The shooter from the car gets out and grabs his gun. He is holding his arm that was hit. Mr. Marcus yells out, "Get in the fucking car. We'll get them on the other side."

Dominique and Paul race down the ally and approach the corvette. Paul says, "We need an opening." Dominique shoots the side window out. A man is walking down the street carrying a bag. You know type, he thinks he's god's gift to women and his corvette is the ticket to their pants. He sees what happened and can't believe it. He yells, "That's my fucking car. What the hell are you doing?" He runs toward the car and sees Dominique standing there. "Hey baby you want a ride you got to let it slide." He is oblivious to the fact she is holding a gun. Dominique grins, "Whatever." She says. He can't believe it. It's his lucky day. "Hell yea baby." He says. Dominique grabs his groin, "You ready?" She squeezes his groin and head bunts him. He stumbles back clutching his noise as blood is rushing out. "What the fuck?" He sputters, as the blood flows between his hands. Dominique kicks him in the chest and he flies into some garbage cans. Paul has now gotten into the car and has had time to hot-wire it. The car carrying Mr. Marcus starts to careen around the corner. Paul yells," Get in!" Dominique opens the door and gets in. The corvette squeals the tires and takes off. Dominique starts to reload her gun. Paul watches in the rearview mirror to see were the black car is.

Paul asks, "You want the scenic route?" He gives Dominique a smile and stomps on the gas pedal. The tires smoke and the car speeds down the street. Dominique, "I just hope this guy has full coverage." She turns around and shoots out the rear window. The black car is now right behind them and closing in rapidly. Both cars are speeding down the road weaving in and out of traffic. The gunman from the black car hangs out the window and starts to fire off rounds. The machine gun is blaring out bullets and pelting the corvette.

The taillights get blown out. The license plate which reads ASSMAN1 goes spinning off as more shots are fired.

Paul looks at Dominique and says, "You going to use that thing?" Dominique inserts a new clip, "Just keep it on the road."

   She points out the back and fires some shots. The rounds pierce the window of the black car, the car swerves and the gunman grabs the hood. He stabilizes himself and fires back. Dominique ducks down behind the seat. The shots from the machine gun rip through the seat inches from her head. The front windshield of the corvette is cracked from the shots. More shots are fired and the windshield gets splattered with blood. It's from Paul's arm which has been hit. Paul screams in pain," hit, I've been hit!" Dominique turns around and fires more shots. The shots hit the gunman and he falls out the window and is run over. The cars are heading for a bridge. The traffic is light as they approach. Mr. Marcus rams the back of the corvette. The car is jolted and the radio gets stuck on blaring thunderous music. Mr. Marcus is at the wheel. Two other guys are in the back. His hands tighten on the wheel. Mr. Marcus, "Hold on motherfuckers, we're sending them off the bridge." Everyone in the car braces themselves. The black car pulls up next to the corvette. Mr. Marcus rams into the corvette. Paul's face grimaces as he tries to hold onto the wheel but his blood soaked hands make it hard to control. Mr. Marcus rams them again this time sending the corvette over the guard rail. Paul grips on to the wheel. Dominique fires her gun at the windshield and blows out some more pieces as the car plummets toward the icy water. Dominique starts kicking at the windshield more and more pieces start falling out. Then the whole thing goes exploding out. She grabs Paul and they crawl out the front window pulling themselves to the top of the car they stand up and jump off. The car smashes into the water they follow behind as the cold water engulfs them and the corvette.

   Mr. Marcus pulls up and gets out. He looks over the edge and smiles. Traffic is stopping as he gets back in the car and leaves. The waves are lapping around in the water as Dominique and Paul emerge up from the abyss. They swim toward the shore and drag themselves up onto the muddy bank and collapse onto the cold wet ground.

Valone Townhouse

Mr. Marcus pulls up and gets out along with the other men. The car is dented and the windows smashed out. They proceed into the house. Valone is in a chair getting a haircut and a shave from a barber. Mr. Marcus walks in and pours himself a drink and sits down. Valone motions for the barber to stop as Mr. Marcus enjoys his victory drink. Valone to the barber, "Thanks Tony we'll finish this later." Tony removes the rowel from Valone and wipes the rest of the shaving cream off his face and then walks out of the room. "Mr. Marcus is my problem solved?" Valone ask. Mr. Marcus replies, "Solved and dissolved, with big black on the attack that bitch was sacked." Valone smiles,"Ah, Mr. Marcus I can always count on you." Valone gets up to leave and pats Mr. Marcus on the shoulder for a job well done. Valone continues, "Enjoy yourself here a few minutes and then we'll head out to the meeting." Mr. Marcus nods and says,"Mr. Valone, I got a question for you." Valone stops and looks at Mr. Marcus. Mr. Marcus continues, "Why do you like meeting in museums?" Valone starts thinking then says, "It's good for us to learn about history. We would hate to repeat our mistakes. We wouldn't want to end up like Desoto, besides it makes a great cover, who would suspect we would meet there." Valone walks out the door and Mr. Marcus nods in agreement as he finishes his drink.

Bankment by the Bridge

Dominique and Paul are resting as they check out their injuries. "You all right?" She asks. Paul responds, "I think I'll live." Dominique continues," We got to get a ride to Gino's building." Paul brushing off dried blood and mud, "I can call a friend, and he's got a car service." He says. Dominique,

"Can we trust him?" Paul take out his cell phone and starts to dial,"Yea, he's legit." The call is answered and Paul say,"Hey this is Paul, I'm going to need a ride, by the bridge, okay great," He hangs up. Dominique," We got a ride?" Paul responds, "Yea, he has a car just down the street." They get up and walk up the muddy hill to the road.

A limo comes down the street and stops. Dominique gets in the back. Paul talks to the driver a minute. He then heads to the back and gets in as the car pulls away. They are resting comfortably in the back as Paul starts to inquire about their situation. Paul asks, "How did you get into all this?" Dominique responds, "Long story." Paul smirks and says, "Long ride." Dominique gives him a look and then starts, "After my mother died and my father was killed Mr. Desoto took me in and we moved to Spain." Paul responds, "Must have been a shock?" Dominique shrugs and continues, "It was, I didn't know anybody and it was all new. I got into a lot of fights at school. That's when Mr. D got me into ju jitsu, so I could protect myself. One thing led to another and I got interested in weapons. He had his top notch guys teach me how to use them. It just hooked me on the lifestyle."
Paul leans back in the seat, "The lifestyle of as pro killer?" he asks. Dominique, "I prefer to call it an angel of death." As she stare out the window. Paul, "That's one hell of a childhood." Dominique agrees and says, "It was, but I had everything I needed. I always felt like I was loved. Long story short I went to work for Mr. D after college, back into the family business as they say. The pay is great but the hazards suck." She looks at the cuts on her arm. Paul concludes, "I hear that." They both smile a tired smile and stare out the windows as the limo speeds along. The sun is setting a bright red orange sunset over the New York skyline and all seems at peace for now.

Brick Building Just Outside the City

From the outside one would think is was nothing more than an old factory. The windows are blacked out with bars on them. A ten foot high fence surrounds the building. Dominique and Paul get out of the limo and walk toward the fence. They start to climb the fence. "You sure you have a key?" she asks. Paul replies, "Yes, it's right here." he starts to tap his shorts pocket. "The gate key must have fallen out when we went for our swim back there." Paul says with a smile. They make it over the fence and head for the building. Dominique surveys the area as they cross the back lot. They reach the door and Paul pulls out the key. He starts to fumble with it to make the key fit. Dominique waits impatiently; she looks at her nails. "Damn I think cracked one, so what kind of toys are going to have for me?" she says. Paul finally gets the key to fit and he opens the door. "Merry fucking Christmas." He says. It's completely dark inside. Dominique and Paul walk in. "What did you get me a piece of coal?" she asks sarcastically. Paul, "Hold on a minute, I'll get the lights." He walks over to a switch on the wall and throws it on. The lights come on and the room is huge. In front of them sits five new black Lincoln town cars. Against the wall sits an office full of windows attached at the end is a brick room. Paul start walking toward the office, "This is Uncle Gino's business equipment, let me show you the real fireworks." he says. Dominique stands for a minute taking in the scene. She then follows Paul into the office.

Three big desks sit inside. The carpet is soft red and a mini bar is in the corner. A steel door that leads to the ammo room sits on the right. Dominique looks at her watch, "The meeting is about to start." She says. Paul looks at her and says, "Let me show you the party favors." He opens the big steel door, inside the room is filled with guns. Assault rifles line the walls a big case in the middle is full of handguns. A box of grenades sits on the floor. Dominique and Paul walk in. "Looks more like an army surplus store in here than an office." Dominique says as she takes down a sawed off shot gun and pumps it. She admires the gun and says, "This ought to wake up the party." Paul comes walking over, "You know our line of work is very demanding, check these out." He takes down two hand machine guns and presents them like fine gold watches, "Their loaded with cop killers and they shred anything." He adds. Dominique takes the guns and inspects them, "Pain is the name of the game." She says as she takes the guns and throws them over her shoulder by their straps. She grabs a bag that sits on the counter and throws in some grenades. "Get the shotgun we're leaving." she tells Paul. Paul looks at her, "I bruise easy maybe I should stay here." he says hoping she will not take him along. Dominique stops at the door, "I'm driving don't worry this time we'll stay dry." Paul smiles and says, "I knew I should have called in sick today." Dominique and Paul head out of the office. They head toward the Lincoln town cars. "The keys in them?" Dominique asks. "Yea." Paul responds. "We'll head back to the town house. I have to get some stuff from my bag." Dominique says.

The overhead door of the building open and the black Lincoln comes out. It slowly gilds from inside the building. Paul," Ah, you remember I don't have the gate key." "That's what the gas pedal is for." Dominique replies. Paul holds on tight to his seat, "This is going to fuck up the paint job." The car's tires screech and the car starts to accelerate toward the gate. The car rams into the gate and the gate flies open, squealing onto the street and takes off down the road.

Museum

A limo drives by and heads around to the back parking area. The streets out front are busy as usual for a Saturday night in New York. The limo pulls up and heads down the ramp which leads underneath the museum. This is the area where exhibits get brought in and out and is off limits to the public. The overhead door shuts behind the limo as it submerges beneath the building. The car stops and a driver steps out and opens the door. Out step Valone and Mr. Marcus. There are six cars already parked. Valone looks around and puts on his suit coat. "Looks like everybody is here." He says. Mr. Marcus comes from the other side and says, "I sent some of the guys over early to secure the area." Valone reaches into the car and pulls out a handgun. "You can't trust this fucking Diablo." Valone says as he checks to make sure the gun is loaded, "He might get some idea in his head that he should be the one taking over. That would be his first mistake." Mr. Marcus pulls back his coat to reveal two 45 magnum handguns strapped to his sides, "His second would be trying to do something about." Valone smiles,"Let's take care of business." The two head down the parking area to the museum which is now closed for the night. They enter through the door.

This part of the museum is a big oval section with high ceilings. In the middle of the room is a huge life size tyrannosaurus rex skeleton. Above it in the roof is a domed window the moon shines through it and pelts of rain gentle run down the side. On the other side of the display a table is set up. Diablo sits on the end with five of his men behind him. On the other side there are six of Valone's men waiting. Everyone is wearing a suit if one didn't know they would think it was a legit business meeting. Valone and Mr Marcus approach the table. Diablo stands up. Diablo speaks, "Vinni sit down, you want a drink?" Valone shakes Diablo's hand and replies, "John where is Gino at? All three of us have to decide on this. The three of our families join together and Desoto will have no juice. We need his men we don't need to be looking over our backs all the time." Diablo responds,"Gino maybe Desoto's cousin but he's all for it he'll be here. Just sit down have a drink and give him a minute." He motions for Valone to sit down. Valone walks to the table and sits down. One of Diablo's men pours him a drink.

Gino's Townhouse

The black Lincoln carrying Dominique and Paul pulls up out front. They get out and head in. Dominique heads to her room. She removes her torn cloths from the earlier action. She just has on her bra and G-string. She starts to get ready to leave. She straps on a wrist knife to her right wrist. On her left she puts on a sliding gun. She tries them both by snapping her wrist and the weapons shoot into her hands. She puts her leg up on the bed and straps a gun to her ankle. She puts on a tight white shirt and some cargo pant then puts on a shoulder holster. Two 9mms sit on the bed, she picks them up and checks the clips and twirls them into the holsters. She grabs some extra clips and puts them into her pants pockets. Dominique then grabs the shotgun she took and pumps it. Paul walks into the room and she turns. "It's time to bring the hurt." She says. The rain is starting to fall harder as they get back into the car and leave.

Museum

Thunder and lightning are lighting up the night sky like a new Broadway show. The glass dome a top the museum is giving the members of the families inside a front row seat. Everyone still sits patiently at the table below. Valone stands up and begins to speak, "Looks like Gino isn't going to show up. Fuck him let's do this. With the blessing of the families I would like to make it official that I will take over operations of the Desoto crime family. No more running around for Sal, we do the business we take the business. What do you say John?" Diablo adjust his shirt and tie then stands up and says, "As one of the three families." Before he can finish the statement a voice is heard. It's Gino, Desoto's cousin. A tall man with jet black hair slowly emerges out of seemingly nowhere with five men behind him. Gino begins, "John, Vinni, I see you guys are still very impatient. What's the matter I crash your little two way fucking party? You guys wouldn't be trying to squeeze me out would ya?" He approaches the table. Gino slowly puts his hand on Diablo's shoulder pushing him back in his seat. Mr. Marcus slowly pulls back his coat. Dominique and Paul arrive at the museum. They sit in the car. "Let me go with you. You'll need some help." Paul says. Dominique replies, "Listen Paul whatever you do don't come in just wait for me across the street. I'm sorry I got you involved but I'm not getting you killed." Paul pleads his case one last time, "What are you going to do walk through the front door? That would go over big." he says. Dominique responds, "I thought I would go to the roof and crash in like a super hero." She gives Paul a wink and grabs the shotgun as she opens the car door. "See you later Paul." she says.

Dominique gets out and closes the door. Paul jumps out the other side with the bag she forgot. "Hey wait." Paul says. Dominique stops. The rain is now a down pour. "Paul?" Dominique asks. Paul throws her the bag and says, "Even super heroes need their capes." Dominique grins as she grabs the bag and fades into the night.

Back inside the meeting is starting to heat up. Valone now interjects, "Let's not have a pissing match here. We all want the same thing Sal Desoto out." Diablo throws his two cents into the now tense situation, "Come on Gino sit down and let's talk about it, get him a drink." He motions to one of his men. Gino contemplates the offer then signals to his men to follow him to the table. He pulls out a chair and sits down. Dominique is at the back of the museum. She approaches the door where the cars entered. The door is closed and she sees a sign above it that reads delivery parking. She looks around for another way. She sees a maintenance ladder that is built into the side of the museum. Workers use it to get on the roof. It's about fifteen feet off the ground so people can't get on it. Dominique notices a dumpster sitting nearby. She walks over to the dumpster and pushes it under the ladder. She climbs on it and tries to reach but it's not enough. She looks around. A side door by the dock opens. It's one of Valone's men who has come out for a smoke. He looks up at the rain falling down and tries to light his cigarette. His lighter keeps going out and he hears a voice. "Need a light?" Dominique says as she comes out of the shadows. The man is startled, "What the fuck? Who are you?" he says. Dominique approaches closer and says, "I'm just working, you looking for a good time?" She snaps her gun out from her wrist holster. The man steps back looking confused he asks, "What the hell that?" Dominique smiles and says, "Relax its just a lighter. What are you working late?" Valone's man looks around and says, "No, no just doing some business, I got to get back inside." Dominique puts her hand on his chest. "How about I lite that cig and then lite this up." She says as she grabs his groin. "Come on twenty bucks I need the money." She says. Valone's man looks around again and checks to make sure no one is watching and replies, "All right hurry up." He covers the cigarette and gun with his hands waiting for the flame. Dominique pulls the trigger. Blood splatters against the wall and he falls back against the door. Dominique kicks his lifeless body out of the way and tries the door but it's locked. She pulls on the door, "Shit!? She says. Dominique grabs the guy and drags him to the dumpster then throws him on top. She jumps up and sets him against the wall under the ladder. Dominique grabs her bag and steps up on the guy so she can reach the ladder. With her shotgun strapped to her back she climbs up through the rain.

Paul has just parked the car. He sits opening a candy bar when he looks out the window and notices a parked car. He squints to see the license plate. He says to himself, "Uncle Gino, that can't be one of his." The windows of the car are starting to fog up so he opens the door and steps out to look. He makes his way over to the familiar car and hears a voice. "Paul is that you? What the hell you doing out here?" Its Gino's driver Joe and he is holding a cup of coffee. Paul looks shocked and replies, "What's going on where is Uncle Gino?"

Joe sips his coffee and replies, "He's inside at the meeting are you late?" Paul stands confused then says, "Yes, hey you still get me in?" Joe puts his coffee down and says,"Yea, come on I got the key to get in, you just in case." Joe gets out and they start to jog across the street toward the back where Dominique went in.

The rain has washed away the blood on the door. It is now raining so heavy they can't even see the body on the dumpster. Joe puts the key in, "Hell of a storm, they're just inside come on." he says. He gets the door open and they walk in.

Dominique is surveying the roof looking for an entrance in. She notices the glass dome and sees a light coming from it. She runs over to the dome and looks in. Below she sees the meeting going on. She sees the men standing around the table looking at each other and pointing. She studies each one of them and stops on Mr. Marcus. Looks like trouble she thinks to herself. Dominique slides down with her back to the dome resting a minute. She holds the bag Paul gave her. Collecting her thoughts the rain continues to fall as she pushes her hair back. She mutters to herself," Twenty people damn, I should have stayed on the beach. What the hell am I getting myself into?" She opens the bag to look inside. Inside are a bungee cord a flare and two grenades. A roll of duct tape plus a .50 caliber hand gun loaded and ready for destruction. She picks up the .50 caliber and says, "This ought to work." Dominique stands up and tapes the gun to her back by wrapping the tape around her waist. She then takes out the chord and walk back over to a steam pipe that extends from the roof. She ties the chord to it and then walks back over to the dome. "This is going to be crazy." She says. Dominique looks inside and notices the men standing up quickly. She wipes the glass to get a better look.
Paul and Joe are walking into the room. Valone stands up; Mr. Marcus steps back and puts his hand on his gun. "What the hell is this? What's going on?" he says. Gino stands up and looks confused and says, "Paul what the fuck are you

doing here?" Paul walks over, "Uncle Gino, I thought you were out of town what the hell are doing here?" Diablo is starting to get visibly nervous and says, "Who the hell are these guys walking in here? Are you setting me up?" Mr. Marcus pulls both of his two guns out and says, "Nobody fucking moves." Valone's men pull out their guns and so do Diablo's and Gino's men. Everyone is pointing at each other as the tension starts to rise.

Dominique continues to watch from the roof. "Goddamn it!" She says. As she sees what is happening. She pulls out a grenade and pulls the pin and throws it through the glass. The grenade gets stuck in the tyrannosaurs rex. "Shit!" She says. Dominique runs back from the dome. Everyone inside looks up as they hear the glass break. Rain and glass come pouring down into the room. Valone squats down and says, "What the fuck was that!" Diablo covers his head and yells, "Just hold on everybody!" As he finishes his statement the grenade goes off blowing up the t-rex and the glass dome. Everyone hits the floor. The bones from the t-rex incinerate into white chip confetti that plummets down onto the men on the floor. The explosion sends debris through the dome as it collapses. Dominique gets up and ties the bungee cord around her ankle and puts on the backpack. She pulls out both 9mm pistols and stars running toward the opening. She plunges head first into the hole.

Smoke is floating in the air. Dominique comes through the opening firing her guns as she spirals downward into the chaos. Two of Valone's men stand up and get shot in the chest. They go flying back to the ground in crumpled heaps. She twists the other way as two of Diablo's men fire. The bullets just miss her. She returns fire shooting one in the head. The other guy gets shot in the neck and falls back holding his throat as it gushes blood. Mr. Marcus sees Dominique. He starts to fire at her. Just as the bullets get to her the bungee cord retracts. She goes flying up. The bullets hit Diablo in the arm and he falls back. Paul throws a chair at Mr. Marcus causing him to go down.

Dominique is now hanging over the table. She snaps her knife out and cuts the chord. She does a flip and lands on her feet on the table where the meeting was taking place. One of Diablo's men lunges at her. She sticks the knife into his throat. Dominique turns the other way and shoots one of Gino's men. She retracts the knife and picks up her other gun. Another one of Valone's men charges, Dominique kicks him in the face. She fires two shots into his chest. Diablo crawls under the table. Diablo looks up and says, "Who the fuck are you?" Dominique replies, "The angel of death." She fires the rest of her bullets into Diablo leaving him a bloody mess. Paul yells out, "Dominique behind you!" She turns. One of Diablo's men is right behind her. She pulls the trigger but nothing comes out. He says, "Dumb bitch." Dominique smiles, she drops the clips from her guns and twirls them around and catches them by the barrels. She then smashes in both sides of his head with the guns. His head busts open like a ripe melon and he falls to the ground. Dominique pulls out he shotgun and shoots the last three Diablo men killing them in their tracks. Now the rest of them realize what is happening. "Get that bitch!" Gino yells as he grabs a gun off of one of his dead guys. Paul runs toward him and yells, "Uncle Gino no!" Gino turns and fires hitting Paul in the shoulder. Dominique turns and pumps the shotgun. Gino aims at her. She pulls the trigger blowing Gino's head right off his body. Mr. Marcus is getting off the floor. He grabs his guns. Dominique looks his way and sees he is about to fire. She grabs the chord and swings off the table with it. Mr. Marcus fires, his shot's miss and hit two of Gino's men killing them both. Mr. Marcus yells"Aaaaaaaaaaaaaah!" He keeps firing at Dominique as she swings toward a cave man display. One of the bullets hit the rope and she drops into the display smashing the glass front as she lands. Valone orders, "She doesn't get out of here alive." Dominique looks at her arm"Fuck!" she says in pain. Blood is running down her arm and her shirt is turning red. She has cuts on herself from the shards of glass. She cuts the duct tape around her waist and removes the .50 caliber. She looks the wounds. She tears the bottom of her shirt off to cover them as best she can. Alone peering through the smoke and debris says, "Come out and make this easy for yourself. Your father didn't put up this much of a fight when I killed him." Valone motions to the rest of his men to move toward the display. Mr. Marcus reloads his gun. They start to creep toward the display.

Dominique looks around to survey the area. She is sitting in a fake cave. Outside stand a couple cave men mannequins with clubs. Dominique checks her guns and puts a clip in one of them. She peers out at the cave and sees them forming around. Valone motions with his finger and says, "In the cave, she is in the cave." Dominique looks out and sees Paul slowly crawling toward a gun. They make eye contact as Paul reaches the gun. He grabs it and fires a shot. The blast hits one of Valone's men in the leg. Everyone turns.
Valone yells," Behind us goddamn it, behind!" Mr. Marcus spins around, "On the ground, he is on the ground." Everyone starts to fire toward Paul. He rolls toward the table and tips it over to hide behind. The barrage of bullets starts to shred the table. Dominique stands up and grabs one of the mannequins between her arms. She extends her arms out so the mannequin's arms are on her shoulders. So it acts as a shield. It looks like the mannequin his running backwards.
She comes running out firing both guns. Dominique unloads into the back of the last two of Gino's men. They drop to the ground. Mr. Marcus turns and starts to fire at Dominique. The bullets pelt the mannequin. Dominique steps back and kicks the mannequin toward Mr. Marcus. The mannequin smashes into him and he falls back. "Ahhh fuck!" he yells. He pushes the mannequin off and looks for his gun.
Valone yells at his two other men as he runs behind a statue "Get her, get her, right there!" Dominique says, "Let's dance boys." She pulls the trigger of the guns but the clips are empty. She drops them. Valone's men smile. Man, "Looks like your luck ran out." He says. They point their guns toward Dominique. She sees her bag with the last grenade sits

between the two men. Dominique says, "I feel sorry for you."
The man replies, "Why is that?" Dominique grins and says,
"Cause this is going to hurt." She snaps her wrist and the
wrist gun slings into her open hand. The gun sparkles in the
light. She winks at them and then pulls the trigger. The
bullets come out as the fire from the gun powder flares out the
barrel.

The bullet hits the grenade in the bag and explodes.
The two guys get blown into pieces. The percussion knocks
over the statue where Valone was hiding. The statue falls on
to him knocking him out. Paul is coming up from behind the
table and yells out, "Behind you!" We hear a gun shot and
Paul falls to the ground. Dominique spins around. She is face
to face with Mr. Marcus. They both stick their guns in each
other's face. The sweat is running off both of their faces. Mr.
Marcus smiles revealing a gold tooth as blood is running from
his nose. "You've been a pain in my ass all weekend." He
says. Dominique responds, "Pain doesn't begin to describe
what you're about to feel." Dominique pulls the trigger but
the gun is empty. She continues to pull the trigger but she
hears is the click of an empty gun. Mr. Marcus shakes his
head back and forth with a grin on his face. Then he says,
"Hmm now that's a damn shame baby. Now I'm going to
have to fuck up that pretty face of yours." Mr. Marcus pulls
the trigger but nothing happens. He is also out of bullets.
Dominique smiles and says, "I should have known. Every
man I'm with finishes early." Mr. Marcus replies, "Big daddy
is just getting started honey." He takes a swing at Dominique
with his gun. She ducks then drives a knee into his gut. He
drops his gun and falls to one knee. Dominique backs away.
"All bark and no bite, come on big man you gotta have more
than that." She says. Mr. Marcus stands back on his feet and
rolls his shoulders and cracks his neck. "All right let's do
this." He says. Dominique starts to approach him with fist
closed. "Just a minute." Mr. Marcus says. "The coat it's
twelve hundred dollar, you mind?" He continues. Dominique
stops as Mr. Marcus starts to take off his long leather coat. He

gets it half way off so his arms are sort of tied and Dominique jump kicks him right in the face. Mr. Marcus goes flying back. He gets up and slowly takes of his coat. He then spits a bunch of blood out. His lower lip is busted wide open. He says, "Ghetto rules hey, I down with that." Dominique responds, "Don't sing it bring it." Mr. Marcus says, "Fuck you."

He swings at Dominique she sides steps and kicks him in the gut. Mr. Marcus spins around. Dominique delivers a series of punches to his face. Mr. Marcus stumbles back his face is bloody. He stands there wobbling. Dominique goes for another punch but it gets blocked. Mr. Marcus punches her square in the face. Blood goes everywhere and she falls back. Dominique is sprawled on her back and it looks like her nose is broken as he face is smeared red with blood. Mr. Marcus comes walking over to where she landed after the devastating punch. He leans over her and says, "All you bitches can give. But you can't take it. When you going to learn you ain't super girl." He stands over her and looks; she has a glazed look in her eyes. Dominique blinks a few times trying to clear the ringing in her head as the blood continues to run from her face.

Mr. Marcus pulls out some brass knuckles from his back pocket and puts them on. "It's time to finish this little dance." He says. He bends down and grabs her by the hair to hold her head up. He pulls back his fist and is getting ready to deliver a fatal blow. Dominique raises her hand near his groin. She snaps her wrist sending her knife into her hand. She jams it into his balls and then pulls it out. Mr. Marcus screams in pain, "What the fuck!" He lets go of Dominique and stumbles back holding himself. Dominique gets off the ground. She removes the knife from the wrist strap. She walks back to the caveman display. Mr. Marcus is trying to crawl away. The blood trail shows where he is going. Dominique comes walking back with one of the clubs from the caveman exhibit. She walks toward Mr. Marcus. She stands in front of him and he looks up. "Tell me something.

Do they play baseball in that ghetto you're from? We played by your rules now it's my turn. You got the balls and I got the bat." She says. Mr. Marcus motions with his hands. He is in extreme pain after having his nuts knifed. "Wait, wait a minute." He pleads. Dominique takes the club and whacks him right in the face. Blood goes flying like rain drops in the night. Mr. Marcus falls back. He tries to get to his knees. Blood is running from his face, one eye is swelled shut. "Looks like that one went foul." She says with a grin. "I better take a bigger swing next time." She continues. Mr. Marcus is on his knees. He raises his head up and spits out a bunch of teeth and blood. He then smiles a big toothless smile at Dominique. Mr. Marcus sits there and laughs from the pain and the fact he knows what is coming. Dominique winds up and lets go, smashing Mr. Marcus square in the face. She steps back as he collapses to the ground dead. Blood pools on the floor where Mr. Marcus lies.

Valone is now conscious he is looking for his gun. His head is bleeding from the statue. He has witnessed what has happened after being dazed. He finds the gun and checks to see if it is loaded. Valone stands up and points at Dominique. "Your father couldn't stop me. You're fucking not going to stop me. This is my business territory and it's my time." He says. Dominique drops the club. She stands there as the rain continues to fall through the hole in the roof. The rain falls like a waterfall from the ceiling as blood drips from her face. She takes her bloody hand and pushes her hair back. "You better not miss." She says. Valone responds, "I didn't last time." Valone starts to pull the trigger. Dominique closes her eyes thinking this is it. Paul crawls up from behind the table with a gun. He fires toward Valone. The shot misses but Valone turns and fires at Paul. The shot hits Paul in the shoulder and he falls down and drops the gun. Valone turns back toward Dominique but she is gone. He looks around in panic. He walks to the center of the room. "Come on you bitch. You fucking bitch!" He yells. He fires some random shots all around. He walks over to Mr. Marcus and looks down. Valone hears a noise by the display and fires some more shots toward it. He sees the display is in rubbles. The glass is all shot up and broken. He sees no movement. Valone feels something hit him and he turns around. It is the rain falling through the roof. He looks up and then turns back around. Dominique comes walking out of the display. She has a bow in one hand and three arrows in the other. She stops and they stand there staring at each other. Valone quickly tries to fire at her but he is out of bullets. "Shit!" He screams. Dominique responds, "Looks like you missed." She loads an arrow. Valone starts to plead, "Think about it. You and me, come on it's obvious you can handle yourself. We can run this city. Anything you want." Dominique looks at him and says, "What I want can't be brought back." Valone frantically searches his pockets for some bullets. Dominique pulls the bow back. She lets it fly. The arrow strikes Valone in the arm that was holding his gun. He drops the gun and clutches his arm. "Jesus, my arm. Can we talk? Come on damn it." Valone pleads again. He wobbles back trying to get the arrow out. Dominique says, "Maybe you're right. Why don't you sit down a minute? We can go over some options." She loads up another arrow and pulls back the bow letting it fly and striking a perfect shot into his leg. The arrow pierces his thigh and Valone falls to his knees.

Valone screams in pain as blood runs from his leg onto the floor. He looks up and sees Dominique loading the last arrow. His eyes blink. His vision is unfocused. His eye sight starts to clear and he can see her pulling back the bow. His eyes shut. Dominique has the bow ready. Sweat and blood are running down her face. She closes her eyes and lets the arrow go. The arrow whistles through the air striking Valone between the eyes. She opens her eyes and sees the rod of the arrow protruding out of his skull as Valone slumps to the floor dead. Dominique drops the bow. She looks up as the clouds have cleared and the moon shines through the hole in the roof.

Valone is bent backwards dead. It looks like he is staring into the moonlight. The light surrounds him like a

spotlight. Dominique looks toward the ceiling. She takes a
deep breath and exhales. She looks toward the floor just
collecting her thoughts and resting from the fight that just took
place.

She is bloody and her cloths torn. Dominique takes
her hand and feels her face softly. The place is in shambles.
Bodies lay everywhere. She hears something and starts
toward the flipped table. Paul comes up from behind the table.
He tears some cloth off his shirt and tries to mend his wounds.
Paul starts, "I never would have guessed Uncle Gino would try
something like this. I thought him and Sal were tight."
Dominique responds, "Greed kills a lot of people. Let me see
your phone. I have to call Mr. Desoto and tell him it's over."
Paul digs in his pocket and pulls the phone out,"Yea, it's right
here." He says as he hands her the phone. She dials the
number and holds the phone to her ear. Dominique says, "It's
me." Desoto responds, "Dominique, I'm glad you're all right.
I take it the mission is over?" Dominique says, "Yes, it's
over." Desoto continues, "I will call Gino, he can start
running things there." Dominique looks down at Gino's dead
body and says, "That might be a problem. It appears Gino
thought he could get in on this and nudge you out. He was
wrong and so were the other." Desoto responds, "I'll fly in
with the boys and straighten out the affairs. I can have a ticket
for you to come home at the airport. You made us proud."
Dominique looks down at her wounds and says, "Don't'
bother; I think I'm going on vacation." Dominique hangs up
and hands the phone back to Paul. Paul says, "You know, I
know some great vacation spots." Dominique smiles and says,
"Paul, I think this time I'll fly alone." Paul smiles. They hear
a noise. Dominique grabs a gun off the floor. It's coming
from behind some rubble that the explosion caused.
Dominique walks toward the noise gun ready. She gets close
and sees Joe the driver. He looks up. "You guys need a
ride?" He asks. Dominique lowers the gun. Paul runs over.
"This is Joe, he's with us. Let me help you up." He says.
"Thanks Paul." Joe responds. Paul helps him up and Joe

dusts himself off. Joe turns to Dominique and says, "I'll bring the car around." Paul chimes in, "I'll go with you." They head for the exit. Paul says, "You know, I'll probably be running things now." Joe responds, "Oh yea, good Gino was a cheap son of a bitch anyways." They walk out laughing. Dominique takes one last look around. She sees Diablo lying there and then looks toward Valone and Mr. Marcus. Smoke still lingers in the room from all of the destruction. She twirls the gun and puts it into the shoulder holster. She says talking to herself," Definitely a vacation, maybe a nice warm beach." She turns and starts to walk out.

The rain has stopped. Dominique comes around the corner of the building and stands on the sidewalk. She looks down the street. Here comes a yellow corvette flying down the road. Rap music is blaring as it approaches. The man inside looks at himself in the mirror he then sees Dominique standing on the sidewalk. He doesn't realize it's her. He squirts some breath spray in his mouth. "Time to pick up some tail." He says as he smiles at himself. He pulls over where Dominique is standing and rolls down the window. "Hey Baby you looking for a good time?" He asks. Before he can finish he realizes that this is the same girl who took his car. Dominique leans over and says, "Ready for the man course stud?" He looks in disbelief and says, "Oh fuck not you, you're one ride I can't even handle." He puts up the window and squeals away as Dominique reads his license plate ASSMAN 2. She laughs as the limo pulls up. Paul is in front. Joe gets out and comes around to open the door. "Boy, that car looked familiar." Paul said through the window. "Just an old friend." Dominique replies. Joe asks, "Miss Sloan, where will you be headed this evening?" Dominique gets in and says, "Home." Joe closes the door and walks back around. The limo pulls away.

The Ambush

The limo starts its journey into the night when Dominique looks up and sees an RPG grenade flying through the air like a firework on the fourth of July. The grenade rips through the front of the limo. Dominique curls up against the seat as the explosion violently echoes through. Dominique's ears are ringing and she can't see. At this point she is barely hanging on to consciences. She starts to hear voices as the smell of gasoline and burning flesh make their way to her nose. She's trying to think but can't. She feels a pull at her legs and the next thing she knows is she has been freed from the wreck. Her hands are quickly tied and a black hood thrown over her head. She can hear the voices but can't make out what language it is. Dominique is tossed into a van as the van speeds away her thoughts turn to Paul and if he is alive.

Remote Area of China

Dominique is starting to regain her senses her blurry vision is now starting to clear. She tries to move but now notices the icy constraints of steel cuffs that hold her to a wall. She can see clear now and looks at her surroundings for the first time in days. The tiny cement line cell which could almost be a dungeon welcomes her with an eerie chill. There are no windows or markings of any kind she frantically tries to figure out what is going on when the steel door starts to move.

In walk four men dressed in black with their faces covered. Behind them walks a short but well-built man of Chinese decent. He has a pencil thin mustache and dark blue suit to match. Dominique thinks to herself," The minute I get free I'm going to castrate this little fuck." The man walks up to her and stares. He signals for someone to bring him a chair. One of the men in black run out and brings one back one setting it down in front of Dominique. The well-dressed man sits down and smiles. "Hello."

He says. His English is good but slightly broken. "My name is Mr. Chin. You don't know me but I know you and I need something from you." Mr. Chin is head of the Chinese mob and he had plans of his own to take over Desoto's power but when he found out about the meeting he thought he would wait to see how it played out. Now he knows and Mr. Chin is ready to go in for the kill. He wants total control of the American organized crime scene. Chin continues, "You see you caretaker Mr. Desoto is standing in my way. So you can make this easy on yourself and tell me where he is and I will let you go." He smiles a friendly smile and Dominique can't believe he thinks she would fall for this bullshit.
"Come on now." Chin says as he taps the side of her face. "Play nice and I won't have to get rough." He continues. Dominique looks down she is wearing an all-white shirt and white pants tied around her waist with a piece of twine. Her feet are bare. She says nothing. Chin gets up and says, "I don't have time for this, you know what to do." He points to the guards and then walks out.

The guards walk over and untie her. She tries to move but feels too weak to fight. They drag her out of the room and down an all-white hall the lights are bright and her eyes aren't use to it so Dominique closes her eyes as she is flung into another room. Mr. Chin is there waiting. "Hook her up he says." There is a machine that looks like a mattress spring standing up. Wires come from the metal springs to the wall. This is some kind of electric torture rack. "Hook her up." Chin says. They slap Dominique against the wire frame and strap her arms and legs. "This could hurt." She says to herself. Mr. Chin walks over to a switch on the wall. "All I want to know is where Desoto is?" Chin says. Dominique looks at him and spits in his face. Chin pulls the switch and electric currents pour through her body causing Dominique to shake violently. The pain is bad but she knows she can't break. "Turn it up." Chin commands. One of the guards walks over to another switch and adjusts the dial. Dominique braces herself for what is to come but it is too much and the pain causes her to black out. Mr. Chin tells the guards to take her down and put her back in the dungeon. "She'll talk." Chin says. "It may take time but she will. Feed her and then in two weeks she'll have enough strength. She'll either talk then or I'll kill her. Either way it'll be done." Chin finishes and walks out.

Over the next two weeks Dominique is fed and allowed to have showers. The accommodations suck but at least they are being human. She thinks she'll have to repay the favor when she kills them. Every time she is allowed a meal it is served with chopsticks and Dominique is now starting a collection. The guards are being lenient with her because she allows them to watch her shower. They have become so enamored with her they even allow her a razor blade to shave her legs. This whole time Dominique has been putting together the pieces and now has a good idea who she is dealing with. The guards have even offered information for extra time watching her shower. If the poor bastards only knew what was coming. Every night Dominique binds the chopsticks together and has been carving them into one large wooden dagger. Her strength is as full capacity on the day Mr. Chin decides to break her again.

One of the guards tipped her off that today was the day so Dominique gathered up the razor sharp pieces of wood and bound them together with the string that was tied around her waist. She now had six inches of death in her hand that was about to be unleashed. She could hear rumblings down the hall so Dominique put the wooden dagger in her waist band. The door opened and the guards lead her down the white hall to the torture room. Once inside they tell her to sit in the chair that is in the middle of the room. A few minutes pass and Mr. Chin walks in. A man follows him who she has never seen. Mr. Chin is dressed sharp as always. He speaks, "So is my favorite girl ready to talk?" He chuckles and then says, "Well I got news for you. It doesn't matter." He starts to laugh. "You see we found out that Desoto is in Monaco. He got a little sloppy after he got to New York and when he left we had no trouble following him." The man who came in with Chin is another Chinese gentleman but a little taller, younger and more athletically built. Chin says, "This is Mr. Hong. He is going to go and kill Desoto for me while I stay here and kill you." Chin motions to the door and says," Mr. Hong, you may go." Hong bows to Mr. Chin and then leaves. Now all that is left in the room is Mr. Chin and four guards. The guards pull the chair out from underneath Dominique and she lands on the floor. They set the chair in front of her and Mr. Chin sits down.

"So you are very quiet, a pretty lady like you should at least have a few last words before we kill you." He flashes a cheap sales man type grin. Dominique gets up to her feet. Mr. Chin looks surprised that she actually stood up. He holds his hands together. Dominique replies, "Your first mistake was taking me. Your second mistake was letting me have chopsticks and your third mistake is sitting where you are." Chin laughs out loud and says, "What are you a fortune cookie?" Dominique pulls out the dagger and impales Mr. Chin in the shoulder before he can even move off the chair. Chin falls to the floor with the wood knife stuck in his shoulder.

Blood seeps from the wound as he lies there in pain. Dominique turns to the guard closes to her and grabs his gun from his holster she quickly shoots him in the face splattering blood across the wall. She turns and fires at the next guard sending a 9mm round into his eye. The other two guards open fire as Dominique drops to the ground and rolls under the table by the spring electrocution machine. She shoots at the switch on the wall and the springs come to life. Sparks swim in the air as the machine is malfunctioning. Dominique searches the dead body of the guard she shot and finds an Uzi machine gun strapped to him. She un-clips it and unleashes wholly hell on the remaining guards shredding them like wet paper in the wind. She gets to her feet and approaches Mr. Chin. She straddles over him and says, "See I had a lot to say." Chin is holding onto the spike which is still impaled into his arm. The pain is so excruciating that he can't talk. Dominique reaches into his coat and pulls out a cell phone and then Mr. Chin's .45 caliber pistol. She sticks the gun to his forehead and says, "Here is a Chinese proverb. You fucked with the wrong person..... asshole." She squeezes the trigger and splatters Mr. Chin's head into a bloody soup of skull and brain matter.

Dominique heads out of the room and it is now apparent to her that she is in a house just outside the city. She starts to dial the phone and hears the other end ringing. "Who is this" a voice replies. "Paul!" Dominique says. Paul responds, "Dominique where the hell are you? We've been looking everywhere for you." Dominique closes her eyes. She is relieved to know Paul made it out alive. She gathers her thoughts as she moves through the house. "Someone named Chin took me and now they're going to kill Mr. Desoto." She says. A different voice this time responds its Desoto, "Dominique, I'm glade your all right. Tell me where you are and we'll come get you." She continues through the house and is now heading down stairs. She can see through the windows that the area is wooded. Dominique finds the front door and opens it.

Three Mercedes Benzes sit out front. She runs to look at the license plates. She looks at them and immediately knows. "China." she responds. Dominique grabs what guns she can and heads out. She gets in one of the cars and knows the plan. Desoto is going to track the phone and find out her location. Then he is going to direct her to a landing strip where a private jet will be waiting to pick her up. Dominique filled in Desoto on Mr. Chin's plans and told him they would be coming. She told him how Chin is eliminated and Mr. Hong will meet the same fate when they meet.

As Dominique pulls out she hears a helicopter coming overhead. The trees start to shake with the force of the propellers. It must have been for Mr. Chin. She accelerates the car and goes sliding down the dirt driveway. She gets about a mile down the winding road when she hears the helicopter coming "That didn't take long, "She says to herself.

The blue and gold helicopter flies overhead. Dominique looks out the window and sees the side door open. Inside the helicopter.50 caliber machine gun is mounted. The bullets start to fly and the red hot shell casings rain down on the hood as she tries to elude them under the trees. The cell phone starts to ring. She answers, "Better make it quick I got some serious trouble." It's Desoto on the other end. "We have your position, I'll have my Burma division send the plane. The landing strip is due south of your location follow these coordinates." He says. Dominique checks the phone and confirms that she has them. "I'll be there." She replies and hangs up. The bullets continue to fly as she darts in and out of the tree line cover.

A clearing is up ahead and she knows her cover will be gone so she darts of the road and down a path. She loses control and the slides down the muddy hill and crashes into a tree. Dominique grabs the Uzi 9mm she took and sprints out of the car. The helicopter starts to descend and lands in the clearing. Two men get out, the pilot and the gunner. Dominique clings tight to the tree, the pilot sees her and opens fire, bark flies from the tree just above her head and she ducks down to return fire unleashing the full force of the Uzi. The gunner and pilot run for cover. "Over there!" The pilot yells.

She slides back down the hill to where the car is and looks inside. She finds a knife. Dominique slides under the car and cuts the gas line. The fuel drains out. She runs back and shoots into the car. The car explodes into a ball of fire, the trees around it singe at the extreme heat. The pilot and the gunman hit the ground. Dominique sees her chance. She sprints up the hill amid the confusion and makes it to the helicopter. She jumps in the side with the .50 caliber machine gun and spins it in the direction of her chasers. "Hey!" She yells. The two men turn and look. Like deer in the headlights they have nowhere to run. She pulls the trigger back and lets the gun do its thing. Thirty seconds and one hundred rounds later The two men get ripped like berries in a blender. She releases the trigger and slides into the driver's side. The helicopter starts to lift off as the clouds of the evening start to drift in.

She makes it to the landing site and puts the helicopter down. She shuts of the engine and waits. A few lights twinkle in the dark sky and she can make out the image of a jet as it speeds toward the runway. The private jet lands on the makeshift tarmac and lowers its staircase. Five well-dressed men in suits are heavily armed as they make their way down the stairs. She recognizes them. A sense of relieve comes over her. This is the first time in a while the odds have been in her favor. The one leading the pack his John Striker, the large muscular man with a cropped hair cut is the very man who trained her. "Dominique?! Striker yells out. She makes her way out of the helicopter and waves so they see it's her. "She's there!" He yells to the others. They run toward her. "Dominique we are glad you're okay. Let's get you on the plane and get you out of here." Striker adds. The men surround her like a package that can't be lost and escort her to the safe confines of the jet.

Monaco- Italy

The sounds of seagulls chirping and the lapping of the ocean water serenade in the air as Dominique's eyes flutter open. She quickly springs up looking for any weapon she can find but then realizes where she is. It's her room at Desoto's mansion. She looks down and sees she is wearing fine silk pajamas, her hands are bandaged and the large bed comforts her as she lies back down. She hears a knock on the large oak door. "Come in." She says. It's Mr. Desoto's butler. The butler says, "It's good to see you in one piece Dominique." She smiles and gets out of bed. "It's good to be in one piece." She responds. "Very good my dear, Mr. Desoto is waiting for you in his office." "Thanks Fernando, you're a welcoming site as always." She says. Fernando smiles. They have known each other a long time and have a special bond. "As you were." He says and turns and leaves.

Dominique walks over to her dresser. The fine marble piece contains a picture of her parents. She picks it up and looks at it as memories flash back in her mind. She slowly sets it down and looks in the mirror. The cuts on her face are starting to heal. She rubs her face and begins to comb her hair. She sets the comb down and takes off her pajamas. She opens a door taking out some tan cargo pants. She slips them on and walks over to her closet and takes out a fine silk white shirt and puts it on. Dominique slips on some shoes and heads out the room down to Desoto's office.

She walks in the door and sees Paul, Mr. Desto, and Striker all talking. Paul sees her and runs over hugging her a little too much, "I never thought I would see you again!" He says as he continues to hold her. This time she lets him. Paul finally let's go. "I'm glad you're okay Paul. What happened that night?" She asks. "Well Joe was killed on impact." Paul says. "I'm sorry." Dominique replies. Paul nods his head in agreement. He continues, "The blast blow the door off and I went flying out and landed on the side of the street. Apparently they didn't see me. I came to just as I saw you being taken. I tried to help but couldn't get up." Dominique pats him on the shoulder and says, "It's okay, I know you tried." Her words comfort Paul who took the whole thing pretty hard. "I eventually got up and out of there then I called Mr. Desoto as soon as I could." Paul says. "We immediately started looking for you." He continues. "We had no idea that Chin took you." Desoto comes over from behind the desk and embraces Dominique. He gives her a hug and kiss, "I thought I lost you." He whispers in her ear. "It'll take more than that to kill me." Dominique replies. Striker comes over and says, "I hate to break up this reunion but we have some business to take care of yet and his name is Mr. Hong." Desoto nods his head in agreement.

Dominique asks, "Who are they?" Desoto pours himself a drink and sits back down and says, "Mr. Chin was the head of the Chinese mafia. That is until he met you. We knew about him but never thought he would try and breach

American soil. The good news is we have intel that the organization is now in disarray and crumbling quickly. The bad news is Mr. Hong who you met is here and ready to strike." Desoto takes a long sip of smooth scotch and leans back. Striker says, "We intercepted their communications and even though the organization is all but finished, Mr. Hong still wants revenge." Striker pulls out a map and continues. "He is here in the harbor about fifteen nautical miles out." Dominique walks over and looks, "So what is the move?" She asks. "I was hoping you would say that." Mr. Desoto grins as he speaks. "We take some men and you me and Striker head out and intercept them right now. No waiting." Desoto says. Paul comes over and says, "What about me?" Dominique walks over to the gun case in the corner and takes out the black benelli automatic twelve gauge with the modified 50 round barrel clip and says "You're with me." Paul smiles and the others grab their weapons and head out.

Mediterranean Sea

The bright summer sun shines like crystal on the waves as Desoto's yacht leaves port. The forty-two foot luxury boat glides across the waves and heads to the danger that waits. Desoto brought along ten members of his personal kill squad. He can take no chances even with his ace Dominique this is a must win situation. "What's the plan?" Dominique asks. Desoto who stands behind the driver smiles and says, "We're going to ram them, just like pirates." Dominique replies, "You got to be kidding me?" Desoto with a twinkle in his eye, "Just be ready to unleash hell on these sons of bitches." Dominique picks up her gun, nods and heads out to the deck. Hong's boat is just ahead. Striker is looking through binoculars and reports, "They see us, their moving on the deck." Desoto tells the captain to pick up steam and ram them.

Hong's boat his equally as nice. The thirty foot luxury boat is holding Hong and fifteen men. Hong who is on the deck can now see the boat approaching fast. He yells out, "Its's them they know we are here!" Desoto's boat is closing quickly. One of Hong's men runs over to him, "What are they doing?" Hong pulling out his silver desert eagle pistol replies, "They are going to ram us." The man asks, "What do we do?" Hong smirks and says, "Let them." Desoto's boat is within striking distance and Mr. Hong yells out, "Open fire!" His men are on the deck with machine guns in hand. The bullets shoot toward Desoto's boat like bees leaving a hive. The windshield spider webs from the shots but doesn't break. "Ram them now!" Desoto yells. The boat clips the front of Hong's boat and the two boats are now stuck together. "Stay and help here Paul." Dominique says as she hands Paul a 9mm. "You got it." He responds. Dominique heads to the front of the boat. Two of Hong's men rush to meet her. She lets go with the benelli pumping four shots into each one ripping their limbs from their torsos. She jumps onto Hong's boat, Striker and the kill squad follows. A fire has erupted at the point of impact and bellows of smoke flow from the wreckage. Mr. Hong sees Dominique. He stands on the upper deck. Striker yells, "Dominique, up top!" She looks as Hong unleashes a direct shot at her. Dominique rolls out of the way and returns fire blasting the upper railing to shreds as the benelli does the heavy lifting. Hong falls back from the violent blast but is unharmed. Dominique sees him sneak inside the boat. "I'm going after Hong." She yells. She kicks in the door to the luxury sitting room just below the captain's port. Hong is just above her.

Outside on the deck the battle continues between Desoto's guys and Hong's. "Paul, get my gun." Desoto says. Paul runs to the gun cabinet and pulls out an over under shot gun and hands it to Desoto. They head out down to the deck. Desoto sees some of Hong's men coming from behind trying to sneak up on his guys so he introduces him to his favorite gun. Two shots ring out as the heads of the two men explode with his accurate shots.

Dominique quietly moves about inside. She starts to make her way up the stairs that leads to the captain's quarters. Instead of opening the door she uses her gun to blow it off the hinges. She kicks the rest of it down and enters the room. As she enters Hong is waiting. He surprises her and tackles her from the side knocking Dominique to the ground. They are now fighting over possession of the shot gun. Dominique quickly lets go and slips her hand into Hong's suit coat taking his desert eagle pistol without him knowing. Hong stands up and throws the shot gun down. "Killing you this way would be too easy." He says. Dominique is still lying on the floor. Hong continues, "I think killing you with my bare hands will be so much more pleasurable but first I might have some fun with you." He starts to remove his coat and Dominique says, "You're wrong, lights out asshole." She pulls out his gun and Hong's face goes white. Dominique pulls the trigger unloading five rounds into his chest. Hong falls back against the controls and slides down. Dominique stands up and walks over to him. She checks the clip, "Ten left." She says. Hong barley alive is looking at her. "What's wrong Mr. Hong? You don't look so well." She says. "Looks like you're a little pale. Maybe you need some lead in your diet." Dominique smiles and unloads the rest of the bullets into Hong. She throws his gun onto the bloody heap that use to Hong and walks out.

The fighting has ended outside. Desoto's guys took a few casualties but in the end they had too much fire power for Hong's men and easily surmounted them. Dominique makes her way to the deck. Desoto is still on his boat yells over, "Did you finish it?" She nods. Desoto, "All right everybody let's get on the life boats and get out of here. The fire is spreading and both yachts are about to be engulfed with flames. Dominique jumps back over to Desoto's and they all run to the life boats and hop in. The three life boats head out as the two yachts explode into a ball of flames.

A yellow cigar boat that was cruising off shore sees the explosion and the two men inside decide to head over.

"I thought I only saw stuff like this back home in New York."
The one guy says. He continues, "Maybe we'll get lucky and
there will be some hot chick we can rescue." The two guys
laugh and high-five each other. The boat races toward where
the boats are coming in. Dominique looks out, "Looks like
help she says." She stands up to look when the guy in the
cigar boat sees her. They look at each other as he gets closer.
His face looks shocked, "No fucking way!" He turns the boat
around and speeds away. Dominique falls back in her chair
laughing as Paul gets up and looks. He reads the name of the
boat as it leaves. He says," Assman three, that's one hell of a
name for a boat."

Desoto's Mansion

The warm sea air fluttered across the tourist woven
beach as the blistering red sun set into the ocean. The evening
light cast large shadows on the towering mansions that
surround the coast. Out on the terrace Mr. Desoto and Paul
are setting up a game of checkers. They are arguing about the
rules. Fernando sets down a bottle of wine for them and they
both agree on that as Desoto opens it. Dominique sits on a
lounge chair overlooking the bay and slowly closes her eyes.
"Anything for you Miss Sloan?" Fernando asks. "No." She
says with a smile. "I'm home. I have everything I need." She
closes her eyes as the gentle ocean breeze drifts over her.

The End